Wish Upon a Pea

Maverick

Chapter Readers

'Wish Upon a Pea'
An original concept by W. G. White
© W. G. White 2022

Illustrated by Marta Orse

Published by MAVERICK ARTS PUBLISHING LTD
Studio 11, City Business Centre, 6 Brighton Road,
Horsham, West Sussex, RH13 5BB
© Maverick Arts Publishing Limited February 2022
+44 (0)1403 256941

ISBN 978-1-84886-863-2

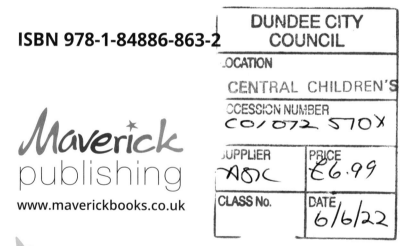

www.maverickbooks.co.uk

This book is rated as: Lime Band (Guided Reading)

Wish Upon a Pea

Illustrated by
Marta Orse

Written by
W. G. White

Chapter 1

This time he'd make it.

John's arms pumped as he ran. The high jump bar in sight, and quickly getting closer. He shut his eyes, launched himself into the air and... whacked his head against the bar.

"Oomph!" he wheezed as he landed on the mat. The bar tumbled down and hit his forehead again. "Ouch!"

The pain wasn't nearly as bad as the laughter of his classmates.

"Okay, that's enough," said Mr Strongarm as he helped John stand. "Not everyone's built for high jump, and that's fine. John here's destined to be an ice skater." Again the class laughed and John grumbled as he stalked back to Nyra. Really, annoyingly tall Nyra.

"You almost made it that time," Nyra whispered as she nudged his arm.

"I hit the bar with the top of my head, I was nowhere near."

John *hated* being small. He was by far the

smallest kid in the whole of Year 4. Maybe even the school! Whilst all his friends kept growing, John hadn't added an inch to his height in at least a year. Nyra, on the other hand, was almost as tall as the Year 6s. She could help Mrs Chesterfield—their teacher—wipe the whiteboard and get books down from the taller shelves. John could barely reach his coat on the hallway hooks.

"Let's go again, John," demanded Mr Strongarm. "You'll be jumping and spinning one day, may as well have the practise."

As the class laughed, John sighed and wished, not for the first time, that he was more like Nyra.

Chapter 2

It didn't matter how much John stretched, he couldn't reach the Choco Puffs.

"Don't worry, John," Dad chuckled as he took the cereal off the supermarket shelf and popped it in the trolley. Such an easy, simple thing for a giant like Dad. "Why don't you go fetch the potatoes? The King Edward ones. Meet me in the frozen section once you're done."

John huffed, stuffing his hands in his pockets as he weaved through the legs of adults. When he arrived in the vegetable aisle, he laughed bitterly. They'd moved the potatoes onto a high shelf.

Even on his tippiest of tippy toes, John couldn't reach the potatoes. And if he could, surely a bag of such heavy vegetables would crush him. No. He needed help.

"Excuse me," he said to a hunched-over old woman with silver-grey hair and a colourful patchwork dress. She wore dozens of necklaces, jeweled rings on her fingers, and a belt with lots of pouches. She was also wearing a bright blue vest with the supermarket's logo and a nametag reading: 'Eileen'.

"Hello my lovely," Eileen cackled. "Need a potion or a lotion? Do you thirst for a curse? Shall I hex an ex? Or maybe charm your... farm?"

"Um," said John, not really knowing what was happening. "Potatoes, please." He again tried to reach the potatoes, showing that he couldn't.

Eileen's eyes flashed. "Ohhh, so height's your plight. Too small to haul your veg-e-ta-bles." She dug into one of her many pouches and pulled out a small tub of something squishy and green. "Peas? Oh please! These are a magical fruit. Mashed to perfection with a wishing lute."

"Peas aren't a fruit," said John.

"One spoonful, here's a clue. One spoonful and your wish shall come true."

Magic mushy peas? How ridiculous. How insane. John wondered if his dad had asked this 'Eileen' to trick him into eating his vegetables.

Yet still... what if it were true? What if he *could* wish himself taller?

John snatched the mushy peas, shovelled not one... not two... but *three* spoonfuls into his mouth and forced himself to swallow. Then he ran. He ran as Eileen shouted after him, **"Thief!"**

He ran through the legs of shoppers and workers, forgetting all about the potatoes. And as he ran, he wished. Just one wish. He only wanted one thing.

"I wish I was tall!"

Chapter 3

When he woke the next morning, John's toes were cold. He peered over his duvet and spotted his feet wiggling out the bottom of the duvet. Heart pumping, John leapt out of bed and snatched a pencil. He stood up straight by the doorframe, where Dad had stuck a measuring tape. John marked his height on the doorframe and stood back.

"I'm 5ft tall!" he exclaimed as he rushed downstairs. Dad was preparing breakfast, but John didn't have time to eat. He'd grown almost an entire foot in just one night. The peas had worked. They'd really *worked!*

At school, John smugly wiped down the whiteboard and reached the high shelves. High jump was a piece of cake, and the look on Mr Strongarm's face as John cleared the bar was worth every spoonful of those disgusting mushy peas.

At the end of the day, John couldn't stop smiling. He and Nyra walked home their usual way, and John was showing off by reaching *everything.*

He stroked cats sitting up high on fences. He reached up and smacked the tall road signs. The world was suddenly in reach and John planned to grab it all.

"How come you're so much taller?" asked Nyra. "Was it just a growth spurt?"

"Yup! Went to bed and woke up tall—nothing to it!" said John. He spotted a tree branch up ahead and got ready to swat it. As he jumped, he felt himself lurch forward and—

Crash! His head throbbed. Rather

than swatting the branch, he'd headbutted it. But how? He wasn't *that* tall... or was he?

"Oh no..." John towered over Nyra. Nyra, who was the tallest kid in school. "Oh no!" That same lurching feeling began bubbling inside of him again.

John was still growing!

Chapter 4

John had to duck to get through the front door, and even then he almost didn't fit.

"John, what's happening?" asked Nyra, who'd followed him home. "You're becoming a giant!"

John could still feel himself growing. The ceiling was getting closer and he had to bend his neck awkwardly. He couldn't stay indoors or he'd grow straight through the ceiling! On his hands and knees, John crawled through the house, into the kitchen where Dad sat reading a newspaper.

"John?" said Dad with confusion on his face. "You're huge, John!"

There wasn't any time to explain. John had to get outside! He pushed through the backdoor and crawled into the garden, where he stood up... and was face-to-face with his bedroom window. But only for a second. Soon, he was peering over the roof of his house. And then down at it. Treetops were getting gradually closer and far, far down on the ground, Nyra and Dad peered up at John.

"I'm so high up!" John felt dizzy looking down. What if he fell over?

Worse still, what if he stepped on someone accidentally? The thought terrified John, so he turned his enormous body and took a single step out of the garden and into the street. Nyra and Dad gasped as the ground quaked with John's stride. Car alarms screeched, windows shattered, and people rushed out of their homes to gawk at the giant boy marching down the street.

As he walked, John dodged birds, telephone poles and trees. He set his sights on a large field at the end of the street. He wouldn't hurt anyone there. At least, he hoped he wouldn't.

Chapter 5

Clouds were wetter than John thought they'd be.
He shivered as droplets of water trickled down
his back. With his head up in the clouds, he could
see the countryside stretching in all directions.
In the far distance, he could even see the sea. On
the ground—which was an awfully long way down
now—Dad, Nyra and dozens of neighbours stood
in the field, staring up at John.

He wished they hadn't followed him. If a stiff breeze toppled him, would he ever stop falling? This must be what skydivers felt like.

A strange buzzing sound vibrated around John's skull. He expected to see a regular bluebottle fly whizzing around him but no... it was a helicopter. The machine's blades chopped and spun as it looped twice around John's head, before stopping in front of his eyes.

Inside the cockpit he could see the pilot fussing over the controls, and a man holding a camera.

Great. He was on the news. Just what every giant boy wanted.

John looked down, and saw scores of black vans and actual *tanks* rolling into the field. Men wearing white lab coats hopped out of the vans, whilst soldiers piled out of the tanks. Before long, they'd built a fence around the field, blocking it off from the neighbours.

Whatever they were doing down there, John hoped they were finding a way to fix him.

Chapter 6

"Giant John, my name is General Furryface of the Royal Army," came a distant voice below. John squinted to see a man with a glorious moustache speaking through a megaphone.

"It's just 'John', actually," John replied in a booming voice.

"Beside me is Dr Bigboffin." The general continued as though John hadn't spoken. "We're going to help you, don't you worry a hair on that giant head of yours."

The army wheeled in a strange-looking machine like a portable tower. The tower extended upwards so it was level with John's face. General Furryface, Dr Bigboffin and a whole bunch of other lab-coat-wearing men and women were standing on the top of the tower.

"We are going to take tissue samples now, yes?" said Dr Bigboffin. The scientists used special tools to take samples of John's hair, saliva, nails and snot. John watched them work, both fascinated and terrified.

"How did this begin?" asked Bigboffin as he inspected a test tube of John's bogies.

"I don't know," John lied. He couldn't tell them he stole the peas! He'd get grounded for sure. Or worse... put in prison. "I just started growing."

"Fascinating."

The scientists worked and John grew. The day stretched into evening, then night, and eventually morning, and John continued to grow. Dad and Nyra visited on the tower, but John was too sleepy to talk. Having them close was a comfort enough.

"We are ready to administer the cure," said Dr Bigboffin, who threw a pellet of something foul-tasting straight into John's mouth. The world stopped and waited. John swallowed the pellet. He held his breath.

And kept growing.

"Disappointing," said Bigboffin. "If we do not correct the growth soon the boy will breach the atmosphere and float away into space!"

Chapter 7

Next, the scientists and the army worked together to create a hodgepodge spacesuit for John to wear. They used parachutes for the bulk of the body pieces, a giant greenhouse dome for the helmet, and whatever other materials the townsfolk were willing to donate. They even got a troop of grandmas to sew the whole thing together.

"John, we need to know how this all started," Dad said from the tower. He and Nyra were wearing their own spacesuits as John reached ever higher into the thinning atmosphere.

"I..." John began. Gosh, he'd be in so much trouble. Not only for stealing the peas but for lying about the whole thing too. If he'd just told the truth at the start maybe they could have found a real cure by now.

But what if he *never* stopped growing? What if he floated away into space, growing forever and ever until he was bigger than the universe itself? What would happen to him then?

He didn't want to think about it.

So he told the truth. Eileen, the peas, the wish; all of it! It all came gushing out of him, the words tumbling over themselves. He couldn't stop now that he'd started, and when he was done, Dad simply nodded and left in search of Eileen.

Chapter 8

The earth curved ahead of John as his head climbed out of the atmosphere. He breathed in deeply, his spacesuit protecting him from the cold nothingness of space.

The tower had climbed with him and there, standing face-to-face with John, was Eileen the supermarket witch.

"Someone got his nasty little wish then," Eileen said as she crossed her arms. She was wearing her own spacesuit, but she'd attached her many pouches to the belt.

"You're not rhyming anymore," was all John could think to say.

"No. I don't rhyme for thieves."

"Can you fix me?" asked John. "I don't want to be big anymore."

"I might be able to. But first you've got to apologise for what you did."

"I'm sorry!" John exclaimed. "I just wanted to be taller! I'll never steal ever again, I promise!"

Eileen narrowed her eyes, then shrugged.

"Alright, I forgive ya. Now, let's put you back to your correct size, shall we?" She dug into her pouches and pulled out a small, plastic tub. Inside was a mushy white paste. It looked disgusting. "Mushy cauliflower, the cure for wishes gone wrong."

"I hate cauliflower," John moaned.

"Well, I suppose you'll be staying giant then."

"No! It's fine... I'll eat it."

Eileen opened the tub and dumped the whole thing into a tube that connected with John's space helmet. Moments later, the horrible, mushy cauliflower was floating around the helmet.

John sucked it all up and immediately felt himself changing… He was shrinking, plummeting through the clouds, the ground rushing to meet him. And then nothing.

Chapter 9

Next morning, John's toes were nice and warm. He stretched and yawned as he pulled back his covers and swung out of bed. His bed. His ordinary, average-sized bed. The mushy cauliflower had worked! He was also very grounded, according to a note from his dad on his bedside table.

John looked out of his bedroom window, remembering when he was tall.

"Hey, John!" Nyra called up to his window, waving enthusiastically. "Do you want to come play in the woods? We're going to build a den!"

"Can't," said John. "Grounded for stealing the peas."

"Oh yeah. Well, see you at school."

Nyra left and John went back to thinking.

He'd enjoyed that one day at school when he'd been tall... but not *too* tall. Before the army and the scientists and space. He shivered, then sighed as he pulled himself away from the window and over to the doorframe and the measuring tape where he'd marked his height. 4ft before the peas, 5ft after them.

Just for fun, he measured himself again.

He gaped, grinning from ear to ear. After all that; the peas, the witch, everything—John *had* grown. He wasn't 5ft, nor was he 4ft. He was exactly 4ft 3 inches. It was only three inches but John couldn't have been happier.

He'd finally started growing! And all it took was a wish upon a pea.

Discussion Points

1. What sport does John do in the beginning?

2. Who gave John the magic mushy peas?

a) Eileen

b) Nyra

c) Dad

3. What was your favourite part of the story?

4. How high does John grow towards the end?

5. Why do you think John ate more than one spoonful of mushy peas?

6. Who was your favourite character and why?

7. There were moments in the story when John **made mistakes**. Where do you think the story shows this most?

8. What do you think happens after the end of the story?

Book Bands for Guided Reading

The Institute of Education book banding system is a scale of colours that reflects the various levels of reading difficulty. The bands are assigned by taking into account the content, the language style, the layout and phonics. Word, phrase and sentence level work is also taken into consideration.

The Maverick Readers Scheme is a bright, attractive range of books covering the pink to grey bands. All of these books have been book banded for guided reading to the industry standard and edited by a leading educational consultant.

To view the whole Maverick Readers scheme, visit our website at

www.maverickearlyreaders.com

Or scan the QR code to view our scheme instantly!

Maverick Chapter Readers
(From Lime to Grey Band)

Pink
Red
Yellow
Blue
Green
Orange
Turquoise
Purple
Gold
White
Lime
Brown
Grey